The Shelter Dog

Written and illustrated
by Christine Davis

The Shelter Dog

Printed in China

Lighthearted Press Inc.
P.O. Box 90125
Portland, OR 97290
www.lightheartedpress.com

ISBN-13:   978-0-9659225-4-8

10 9 8 7 6 5 4 3 2 1

This book is dedicated to
all the loving critters
waiting in animal shelters
for their forever families
to find them.

And to all the special people
who care for animals in
need....a heartfelt thank you!
Whether you work alone,
or with shelters or rescue groups,
you are truly angels.

Hero was having a perfect day, flying through the heavens with the other angel dogs. They soared above the clouds and around the stars, stopping whenever a field of soft grass or brilliant flowers beckoned to them.

Then they would drift down
and float among the petals,
sharing stories of the lives they
had lived when they had been
dogs on earth.

Hero had a clear memory of his earthly existence. He had been the companion of a young girl who wasn't able to run and play like her friends. So, she and Hero would play together, he racing to fetch a ball or toy then prancing back to her side with his head held high. A glowing circle of light always seemed to surround Hero, but only the girl could see it.

"You are my Hero," she would say, holding his head in her hands as his tail wagged furiously back and forth. And Hero would gaze into her laughing eyes...eyes that were the color of the sky...and know that he was loved.

Time has no meaning when you live in the stars. Hero really didn't know how long ago this had happened. He just knew he had been very happy on earth. Not all the animals he met had known that same happiness. Some had never found their forever families. Others had known illness and had left the earth when they were still young.

But it was the ones that had been adopted from animal shelters that captured Hero's attention. They had been rescued by very special people, who welcomed the homeless creatures into their families where they were loved for the rest of their lives.

Hero thought a lot about being adopted. It must be wonderful to be a shelter dog and have someone find you and bring you home to live with them. One day, he asked the Shelter Angel, who watches over all the animals that are up for adoption, if he could go back to earth and become a shelter dog.

The angel saw all the hope in his eyes. After all, he had only known love, both on earth and in the heavens. "Hero," she said, "not all the animals that are up for adoption find the happiness you have heard about."

But Hero's unwavering faith touched the angel's heart. "I'll be watching over you," she said, as she disappeared into the evening sky. Suddenly, Hero found himself tumbling, tumbling, down through the stars, through the clouds, until he landed softly on the ground.

When Hero opened his eyes, he saw he was in a small room with a gate in front. He tried to stand up, but he was very stiff, and one back leg didn't work the way it should. Something must have happened on the way down, he thought. Perhaps he had hit the ground too hard. But Hero wasn't worried. After all, he had been an angel dog and had been sent from the heavens to experience the joy of being adopted. Surely a loving family would want to bring him home.

Hero pulled himself upright, and wobbled to the gate on three legs. Two shelter workers came over to see him, reaching in to scratch his head. "Poor old boy," one of them said. "He just showed up, no collar or tags, wearing an old bandana."

"One of his back legs isn't quite right, either," said the other one. He offered a rubber ball to Hero, who took it playfully in his mouth and tossed it into the air. "Still, there's something special about this dog. I hope people will see that."

It wasn't long before the doors opened and visitors began walking through the shelter. Hero stood by the gate, anxious to meet the person who would want to adopt him. But people looked briefly at his old face, and the back leg that jutted out to the side, and kept on walking.

Hours went by, but no one was interested in Hero. Soon it was time for the shelter to close. Many animals had been adopted that day, and Hero's generous heart was happy for them all. Tomorrow would be a better day for him.

The next day, Hero was standing by the gate
again. This time, he carried the ball in his mouth,
ready to greet each person who came down the
corridor. But all the visitors passed him by. Day
after day, Hero stood by the gate, certain THIS
would be the day he would go home. But every
day ended like the one before.

$\mathcal{S}$everal weeks went by, and Hero was beginning to lose hope. It was harder and harder for him to pull himself up on his three good legs, so he spent most of the time in the corner of his room. He no longer looked up when people walked by. The rubber ball lay forgotten on the floor.

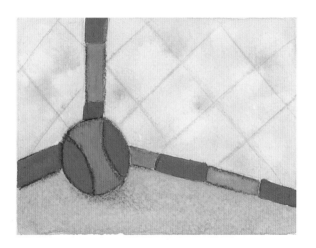

Hero began to hear words like "If someone doesn't adopt him soon" or "We'll give him until Saturday." Up in the heavens, where he had been happy and loved, there was no such thing as time. But it was different on earth...and Hero knew he was running out of time.

The week rushed by, and Saturday came. The shelter was crowded with people looking to adopt an animal companion. Hero was curled up on the floor when a family with a little girl stopped at his gate. The child knelt down and put her hand out toward the dog. Perhaps this was the family that would rescue him and bring him home.

Hero pulled himself up on his rickety legs and hobbled over to the outstretched hand. The child stroked the old dog's head, then looked up at her parents with hopeful eyes. But they had seen how hard it was for the dog to stand, and they looked with concern at the back leg dragging behind.

"No, honey," the parents said. "Let's keep looking."

The family walked away, taking with them Hero's last chance for being adopted. He limped back to the corner, where he lowered himself to the ground and closed his eyes. He knew that soon he would be an angel dog again, flying through the starry skies.

"Here's where we keep the dogs that are up for adoption, Aunt Grace." Hero recognized the voice of one of the shelter workers. "I need to go lock up for the day, but you can take a quick look around if you like."

From far away, Hero heard a shuffling sound moving slowly down the corridor. It would have been nice to see one more person before his time on the earth was over. But Hero's heart had never felt so heavy. He was going to leave this life without understanding why no one had wanted to adopt him.

The shuffling sound was getting closer, but Hero no longer had the strength to care. He lay on the floor and thought about all the heavenly friends who were waiting for him.

The shuffling sound came to a stop.

"Well, hello there, old boy."

Hero slowly opened his eyes. A woman was sitting on the bench outside his room, holding a cane in her hands.

"Would you like to come over and say hello?"

Hero could feel the kindness in her voice. He wanted to go to her and offer his heart one last time. What if she was the one who had come to bring Hero home? What if there was a special place on her bed that was meant just for him? What if she was his forever person – the one who would understand about angels and flying through stars and landing in fields of flowers?

But Hero didn't move, because his heart could not bear to watch another person turn and walk away from him.

"It's all right," the woman whispered, as she made her way around to the gate in front. "I'm old, too."

Hero looked up at the woman. Her words reached out and touched the brokenhearted dog. He came awkwardly to his wobbly feet and slowly approached the visitor, dragging his back leg behind him. Something about her made him think of long ago days. He felt at peace in her presence.

Hero gazed into her face. There was something familiar about her eyes. They were older, now, but…he KNEW those eyes… laughing eyes… *eyes the color of the sky*!

Suddenly, Hero's heart began dancing inside him. He was so excited he could hardly stand still. Happiness spilled out of the heavenly dog and filled the room around him. His tail wagged furiously back and forth.

He was going home!

"*W*oof!" he barked, putting his head through the gate and nudging the woman's hand. Then he limped to the corner and picked up the ball, returning to the door as fast as his three good legs could carry him. His knowing eyes never left the woman's face. And then something amazing happened. *Hero began to glow!*

The old woman looked at the joyous creature, standing in the circle of light. She could see all the love in his hopeful heart. Memories from long ago washed over her, and all of a sudden she KNEW who it was that stood on the other side of the door!

The gate was opened and the woman slowly dropped to the ground, gathering the old dog into her arms. She didn't know how this could have happened. She didn't need to know. "You are STILL my Hero!" she cried, as tears ran down her wrinkled face.

HERO

Hero stepped into the corridor,
taking his place next to the woman
who had come to bring him home.
They walked out together, she
leaning on her cane, he limping
along on his three good legs.

*That night, there was a peace in
the shelter that was felt on earth
and throughout the heavens.*

*A*nimal shelters are overflowing
with critters who are waiting for
loving families to find them.

Be a HERO –
open your heart and home to
a shelter animal.